# Death
in the
# Gardens

by

John Messingham

Copyright © 2025 John Messingham

All rights reserved

The characters and events portrayed in this book are fictitious. Any similarity to real persons, living or dead, is coincidental and not intended by the author.

No part of this book may be reproduced, stored in a retrieval system, or transmitted in any form or by any means, electronic, mechanical, photocopying, recording, or otherwise, without the express written permission of the author.

Cover design by John Messingham

Lily and Bob

# One

"It's good to see you moving on. I know the divorce was a horrible time for you and has not left you with much, but I am not sure trying to get more money out of the boss is a good idea."

Hannah listened intently to what her friend Amy was saying but knew she was not going to change her plans on anyone's advice. She was in a lot of trouble financially and was trying to sort things out the best way she could think of. Once Amy had finished giving Hannah her thoughts, Hannah said.

"I know what you are saying but I cannot think of anything else to do, and, let's face it, I'm not taking anything from him that he has not stolen in the first place."

Amy thought for a moment about what Hannah had said and replied.

"That's true but remember the other person involved is dangerous and would not think twice about hurting you, or worse."

After this exchange, the two girls sat in silence while they finished their meal and when they had finished, Amy looked at one of the waiters and indicated she wanted the bill. As she did, she said.

"I'll get this one."

They chatted some more while the waiter processed Amy's credit card payment for the meal, and on completion, they both got up from the table. Another waiter brought their coats back to them from where they had been hanging on a coat stand in the corner of the dining area and held them both out towards the women. Amy took hold of hers and started putting it on while the waiter, now only holding Hannah's, held it open behind her so she could slip her arms into the sleeves.

Once they had both finished fastening the coats, they made their way towards the restaurant door, and as they approached it, one of the waiters opened it for them. Amy smiled at the waiter holding the door and said as they went through it.

"Must be a slow night tonight to be getting all this attention."

*****

Once outside the restaurant, Amy and Hannah stopped, and Amy said.

"I hope you will think again about what you are doing."

Hannah looked at Amy and, after thinking for a moment, said.

"I don't think I can because I cannot think of another way to get sorted out. But thanks for tonight, I've enjoyed it."

Amy stared at Hannah and said.

"Well, if you ever need help, call me."

Hannah nodded and held her arms out. Amy moved forward, and as Hannah embraced her, she returned the hug. After a few seconds, they moved apart and, after watching for a gap in the traffic started to cross the road. Once across, they both said their goodbyes and parted, both walking in opposite directions. Amy had parked her car along the main road towards the Pier whereas Hannah had left her car down on the Promenade which meant walking further up the road and through the formal gardens that lay between the road they had just crossed and the lower road that ran alongside the central promenade.

As Amy arrived at her car, she looked back and saw Hannah entering the gardens in the distance, so she went round to the driver's side of the vehicle and once she was sure no cars were coming unlocked the car with the key fob and opened the driver's door. Once she was inside the car, she put her bag down on the passenger seat and sat for a few minutes thinking, before starting the car's engine and pulling away to make her way along the road towards her home. As she passed the entrance to the gardens where she had seen Hannah going through, she looked for her but it was too dark to see anyone or anything moving.

*****

Inside the gardens. Hannah was walking along one of the footpaths that led through the area and towards one of the paths, leading down to the promenade. As she walked, she thought about what she had just been talking to Amy about and what she hoped would make a big difference to her life. It was at this point she heard someone running behind her. She assumed it was a jogger, because many people took the opportunity to run along these paths in the darker evenings, as there were less people about to have to avoid. As she prepared to move out of the way she turned her head slightly to see where the person was, but as she looked back, she realised the person coming towards her was not wearing the usual brightly coloured clothing joggers wore but was dressed in very dark clothes.

Realising the person behind her was heading directly towards her, Hannah turned and started to walk quickly towards the path she had been heading towards. But she was not quick enough and she soon felt herself being grabbed from behind. She was just about to start screaming but as she opened her mouth she felt a hand coming over it and press tightly against her face. It was not long after this that she stopped feeling anything at all.

# Two

"Morning, Sir."

Brierton greeted Garner as he approached the line of plastic tape stretched across the path leading to the cascading waterfall with the large concrete Pelican overlooking the South promenade in Cleethorpes.

He acknowledged Brierton's greeting with.

"Morning, Becca, you're up and about early. I thought you would have been struggling after your night out. Which I hear was eventful."

Brierton smiled and replied.

"Not sure what you mean, sir. It was just a few drinks after finishing my exams."

Garner bent down to continue under the tape that a uniformed officer was holding up. Garner thanked the officer, and once he was closer to Brierton, they both made their way towards the waterfall, where there was much activity. As they arrived, a white-suited person turned towards them and said,

"Oh, it's you. I was hoping Becca would be leading on this one."

All three stood silently for a moment, and then the person in the white suit lowered their face mask to reveal it was Rachel Howton. Rachel had been assigned to the case as the Crime Scene Manager. Garner asked.

"Do we have an ID for the victim?"

Brierton replied.

"Yes, we found a council photo identification card in her pocket. The details on the card suggest the victim is Hannah Finley."

*****

Howton looked towards Garner and Brierton and said.

"Morning you two. How are you both?"

Brierton replied.

"Fine thanks, you?"

Howton laughed and replied.

"I was OK until I got called out here and ended up in the bloody pond."

Garner looked round and asked.

"What's happened? I was told a body had been found at the bottom of the waterfall."

Howton walked forward and stood in front of Garner and then turning to look back towards the waterfall said.

"Would it really hurt you to exchange pleasantries in the morning?"

Garner looked at Howton and laughed before saying.

"I was not coming in until later today but got called about this. You have no idea how painful life is until I've had at least two teas."

Howton shook her head and then pointed towards the large concrete Pelican statue in the pond at the bottom of the waterfall. As she did, she started to talk.

"The council guys came along to do their normal morning checks and start up the waterfall but as the looked around they saw the body lying in the water, so called us."

Brierton took a few steps towards the waterfall and looked at the pool of water at the bottom and said.

"I bet it gave them a shock. I bet the worst they have seen until now was the pond full of soapy water."

Brierton walked back and stood beside Garner, who said.

"What about the body?"

Howton started to walk towards a small tent that had been erected in front of the waterfall. As she did Garner and Brierton followed her. Once at the tent, Howton went inside and again Garner and Brierton followed her.

*****

Inside the tent there was a young female lying in an open body bag with a member of Howton's team taking some last photos of the body.

Howton looked at the photographer and said.

"Can you give us a moment?"

The photographer looked at Howton and quickly left the tent.

Garner lent towards Brierton and whispered.

"Crikey, they didn't need to be asked to get away from her twice."

Once Howton was standing on the other side of the body she knelt beside it and started to speak.

"It looks as if she was attacked above the waterfall because we found some fibres similar to her clothing on the railings above the waterfall. I won't know for sure the time of death until later."

While he was looking at Howton and the body, Garner asked.

"Are you sure we are dealing with a murder scene? And not just an accident where she was maybe playing around at the top and fell over the fence."

Howton looked up at Garner and replied.

"There is a lot of bruising on the body. Most

of it fits in with falling down the waterfall but there is some bruising around her neck that seems a bit out of place. So, I will need to get her back to the mortuary and carry out a full post-mortem before I can be sure. But my gut feeling is that this is not an accident."

Brierton said.

"Are you saying you think she was dead before going down the waterfall?"

Howton got back up from her knees and said.

"My initial examination of the body suggests just that."

*****

Up in the area above the crime scene, officers could be heard moving around within some bushes. They had been searching the area for hours now and were making one final sweep of the area just in case something had been missed. It turned out that something had indeed been missed because one of the officers came out of the bush and called over to the search coordinator.

"Sarg, I have got something here."

All the other officers nearby looked up to see what was going on. Seeing this, the Sergeant coordinating the search bellowed out at all the other officers searching.

"Keep searching, looks like we missed something the first time."

The Sergeant moved quickly to where the other officer was standing and once he had joined them, he said.

"Right then, what you got?"

The officer pointed back into the bush and said.

"There's a small bag with a long strap hanging in one of the bushes through there."

The sergeant looked past the officer and into the bush but could not see the bag so took a couple of steps forward which then enabled him to confirm what the officer was saying they had found. He stepped back from the bush and said.

"OK, well spotted. Stay here while I call the crime scene guys who are still here to come and have a look."

Leaving the officer guarding the location of the bag, the Sergeant took hold of his radio and called back to the stations control room. Once he had spoken to the control room staff he returned to the other officer and told him what was going on. He said.

"OK, we'll wait here. One of the crime scene staff is heading up here to have a look at the bag."

The two of them just stood in silence while they waited.

*****

Until they examined the contents, there would be no way of knowing if the bag belonged to the victim or not. So, once the crime scene team who had arrived and photographed the bag where it had been found, it was brought out of the bushes and placed on a plastic sheet that had been laid out on the grass. It was then opened and the contents removed one item at a time. The main items brought out of the bag from the investigations point of view where a mobile telephone, a set of keys, which contained a various assortment of keys, one of which was a car key. The other item of real interest to the police was a driving license. This confirmed the bag belonged to the victim because the license had her name and photo printed on it and what was going to be a real help now, was that it also had an address printed on it.

The Sergeant noticed the licence being laid down on the sheet so stepped forward and said.

"Can I copy that, so I can send a copy of it to DCI Garner."

The crime scene guy replied to this request by holding up the licence between his fingers so the Sergeant could use his mobile phone to photograph the card. Once he had done this and checked the image was sharp, he said.

"Thanks. I'll call DCI Garner and let him know what we have found. I think he is still here so he may pop up."

The crime scene guy said.

"OK. Seeing as there is a car key here, I'll get onto the station and get them to look up the details of any car registered to her. It may be around here somewhere."

As the Sergeant listened, he was also looking at his phone to get DCI Garner's number ready to call and as he walked away, he tapped on his phone to initiate calling. As the call seemed to be answered, the Sergeant walked a short distance away from the others and spoke to Garner and after a few moments, returned to the others and said.

"Right, DCI Garner has told me to get the phone sent to the station for analysis."

Hearing this, the crime scene team member picked up the phone and after placing it in an evidence bag and writing the details on the outside of the bag, passed it to the Sergeant. Who, in turn said.

"I'll get this sent to the station."

# Three

Brierton led the way into the council offices with Garner following closely behind her. As they arrived at the reception a young man looked up at them and said.

"Hello, can I help you?"

Brierton paused for a moment while Garner moved next to her and then she replied to the receptionist.

"We would like to speak to someone about Hannah Finley, please."

The receptionist moved her attention to her computer and after a couple of clicks of her mouse looked back up and said.

"I'm afraid Hannah is not in this morning. Looking at her diary, she should be here but she does not appear to have signed in yet."

Brierton looked at Garner briefly and then looked back at the receptionist. She said.

"We know she is not here. We would like to speak to her boss or line manager."

The receptionist replied.

"Sorry, yeah, hold on. I will call her manager."

The receptionist once again looked at her screen and after another couple of clicks, paused, and then started speaking into the microphone attached to the headset she was wearing.

"Hi, there are some people here wanting to speak to you about Hannah Finley."

She paused again while the person on the other end of the call was obviously speaking and then the receptionist looked at Brierton and asked.

"Sorry, I should have asked. Who are you?"

Both Brierton and Garner took their warrant cards out of their pockets and held them up.

Garner said.

"I'm Detective Inspector Garner and this is Detective Sergeant Brierton."

The receptionist looked at bit embarrassed. This was more due to having not checked who Garner and Brierton were than having not asked in the first place. She spoke into her microphone.

"They're the police."

*****

After about ten minutes Hannah's boss arrived in the reception area of the council offices were Brierton and Garner were waiting. She approached the pair of them and asked.

"Are you the police officers asking about Hannah?"

Brierton looked at the woman and holding up her identification so the woman could see and read it, said.

"Yes. We are?"

The woman who was clearly not happy about being summoned to the reception replied quite sternly to this question.

"I'm Amy Strong. I'm Hannah's line manager. What is this about?"

Garner moved forward and stood next to Brierton. He had very quickly got fed up with this woman's attitude. Brierton realised this so quickly started to explain why they were there.

"I'm sorry to say that Hannah was found dead this morning in what are very suspicious circumstances."

This had the desired effect on the situation and not only stopped Garner from stepping in and saying something but clearly shocked Amy to the point where she looked as if she was going to fall over due to her legs wobbling beneath her.

Brierton said.

"Would you like to sit down?"

Amy looked at her and then at a chair next to her and started to sit down as she nodded at the offer.

Garner looked over to the receptionist and asked.

"Can we get some water over here please?"

*****

The receptionist passed the small cup of water she had got from the dispenser in the corner of the reception to Amy and then went back to her desk. Amy drank from the cup and once she had composed herself looked up at Brierton and asked.

"Sorry about that. I was not expecting you to say anything like that because we had a meal in Cleethorpes last night."

Brierton said.

"That' OK. It's never easy news to hear."

Brierton thought it best to give Amy another couple of seconds to gather her thoughts but was also aware that Garner would want to get moving on questioning Amy about Hannah so they could start to build a picture of her recent movements and dealings with anyone in the workplace that may have a bearing on what had happened to her. So, as soon as she thought Amy would be ready to talk, Brierton said.

"Is there somewhere we can go to speak where it is a little more private?"

Amy looked over to the reception desk and said.

"Can you give these officers some visitor badges? We can then go through to my office."

Amy, Brierton and Garner then waited where they were until the receptionist came from behind the desk and walked over to them. There she gave both Brierton and Garner a visitor pass which they duly clipped onto their tops. Once they were ready, Amy got up from her seat and walked towards the door that led into the office area behind the reception area of the building. Followed by Brierton and Garner.

*****

As the three walked into Amy's office, a man who was sitting on a chair just inside the door stood up.

Amy said.

"Oh, your still here."

The man grabbed a jacket hanging on the back of the chair and replied.

"I'll get going then if you're busy. Will I see you later?"

Amy walked across to the man and gave

him a hug and kiss on the cheek. She grabbed a bright woolly hat from a small table beside the chair where the man had been sitting and put it on his head, saying.

"Don't forget your hat. It's cold out there."

The man adjusted his hat to sit properly and then started to leave the office, only acknowledging Garner and Brierton's presence by nodding to each of them in turn as he passed them and left through the door. Amy went around her desk and sat down. Brierton walked towards the desk and said.

"Is that your husband or boyfriend?"

Amy looked at Brierton and gave out a little laugh. She followed this by saying.

"Sorry, I shouldn't laugh after the news you just gave me about Hannah but, no, that's Freddy. He has his uses, if you know what I mean, but he's a bit like Blackpool. OK for the weekend, but you would not want to live there."

Amy paused for a moment and then said.

"Right, how can I help you."

Garner had now made his way to the front of Amy's desk and asked.

"What was Hannah's role here at the council?"

Amy replied.

"Well, she is, sorry I mean was Albert Burke's personal assistant. He runs the buildings department so will probably be in his office. I was Hannah's line manager so only really saw her now and then if there were any employment issues. But it was rare for me to have any dealings with her in work. We were friends outside of work so probably had more contact with her away from the office."

While Amy was speaking, Garners mobile started to ring so he took it out of his pocket and looked at the screen. He could see it was Rachel Howton calling so he answered the call and said.

"Hello Rachel."

While Garner was taking his phone call, Amy looked at Brierton and said.

"You'll probably want to speak to our head of finance as well. Hannah assisted him from time to time because she used to work in the finance department."

Brierton made a note of this and asked.

"Right, what's his name?"

Amy replied.

"Victor Glenn, I know he is out at meetings today but he should be in his office either later today or in the morning."

Brierton added this name to her notes and then turned her attention to Garner who was still on his call.

*****

Garner was listening intently as the caller spoke and then he said.

"OK, thanks, I'll get DS Brierton to come down and meet you. Speak to you later."

Once he had ended the call and replaced his phone back into his pocket he looked at Brierton and said.

"That was the crime scene team. They are at Hannah's flat so can you go down and meet them?"

Brierton nodded and replied.

"OK, I'll head down there now."

Garner said.

"Right, before you go."

Garner then looked at Amy and asked.

"Do you know if Hannah had any relatives? We looked up her details but couldn't see any."

Amy quickly replied to this question.

"No, she had no relatives as far as I know. I seem to recall that when she was asked for next of kin details when she started working here, she said to stick me down as we had known each other for a while."

Garner turned back to Brierton and said.

"OK, head down to the flat. See if there is anything there that confirms she had no family."

Brierton smiled at Garner, nodded in acknowledgement of what he had asked Amy and then left the office as Garner asked Amy.

"A couple of questions I need to ask. Can you think of anyone who may want to harm Hannah? And can you point me towards Mr. Burke's office?"

*****

Amy thought for a moment and then replied to Garner's first question.

"No, no one comes to mind. I know she went through a horrible divorce last year and there has been some wrangling regarding the settlement. I think there was a prenuptial agreement worth a lot of money but I wouldn't have thought her ex would do something like this to her."

Garner made some notes in his notebook and asked.

"Right, can you give me her husbands name?"

Amy replied.

"Yeah, it's Travis Blackburn. I'm not sure where he is living nowadays but I doubt it will be far from here as his businesses are mostly based in the area."

Garner made a note of the ex-husbands

name and then asked.

"That's fine. If you can point me to Albert Burke's office. I'll leave you in peace."

Amy smiled and said.

"That's OK, I'll take you there."

They then headed out of the office and as they made their way to Albert Burke's office, Garner said.

"You said you had been with Hannah for a meal last night."

Amy replied.

"Yes, that's correct."

Garner said.

"What time did you leave the restaurant and did anything unusual happen as you parted?"

Amy stopped and turned towards Garner. She said.

"Nothing, we finished eating just before nine, I paid for the meal and we went our separate ways. I saw her enter the Pier

Gardens but that was it."

As she finished speaking, she started to walk again and they soon arrived at and entered the office of Albert Burke.

# Four

Inside Hannah's flat, uniformed officers were in every room, searching through every drawer, cupboard and shelf within. A crime scene manager had been there before them, and after carrying out a thorough check of the property, was happy and had declared it was not a crime scene. Brierton had gone on ahead of Garner as she often did to oversee the search and to help gather everything found that may be useful to the investigation. As she entered the flat, she noticed a large plastic box containing some evidence bags sitting near the entrance door with a uniformed officer standing guard. She flicked through the bags to see what had been found. As she did, she heard a voice calling from a doorway further along the flats entrance hall.

"You'll want to see what we found in here."

Hearing this, Brierton started to walk along the hallway to meet with the other officer who had called out to her. At the same time, one of the more senior officers present appeared from a room and said.

"Hi there, do you want to take this one?"

Brierton looked at the officer and replied.

"Can do, have you found anything useful?"

The uniformed officer held up a couple more evidence bags and said.

"Maybe. I'll speak to you about it when you're ready."

She nodded and carried on walking towards the room the previous call had come from and as she entered the room, she could see straight away it was a bedroom. Standing in front of a large wardrobe, standing against the wall opposite what looked like a king size bed. The officer said.

"Here, look at this."

*****

She walked around the bed and as she arrived at the wardrobe door, the officer opened it fully and moved out of the way to allow Brierton to look inside. As she looked inside the wardrobe, she saw that all the clothes had been pushed to one side and a tall piece of wood was leaning against the back of the wardrobe. She could also see some shelves to the side of the main compartment. She looked at them and then back around the door which she was holding and could see there was a mirror on the outside of the wardrobe, in front of the shelves. She looked at the officer and said.

"Good work. How did you spot that?"

The officer replied to her question.

"It looked like that side was quite a bit narrower than the actual wardrobe front, which seemed a bit odd. When I moved the clothes along the rail I could see there was a gap at the back of that panel. So, I pulled the panel out and it revealed those shelves and what you can see on them."

Brierton turned her attention back to the inside of the wardrobe and started to look at the contents of the shelves.

On the top shelve was a small, modern video camera. The type used by people who make videos to post online. The camera was on a small tripod which was fixed to the shelf. This suggested the camera was in the position where it would be used. As she studied the camera and its position the officer in the room with her said.

"I have looked closer and the mirror is a two-way one. I am guessing the camera was used to video the bed and, well, whatever took place there."

Brierton looked at him and said.

"I guess so. Take some photo's of how this is all setup and then bag it all up so we can look at it later."

As she started to leave the room, the officer who was using his phone to take photographs of the wardrobe interior said.

"Look at this."

As he spoke, she could see him holding a small plastic box and walking towards her. He held it up so Brierton could see it and read what it said on a sticky label that had been applied to the lid and said.

"It looks like a box of memory cards. We can only guess what is contained on them at this point. but the label says, Victor and Jenna Glenn."

Brierton looked at the box being held up in front of her and replied.

"I think we can guess what is on them. Bag them up and we will look through them back at the station."

# Five

Albert Burke was sitting behind a large wooden desk reading some paperwork when Amy led Garner into his office. She said.

"Albert, sorry to bother you but I have detective Inspector Garner with me. He needs to speak to you about Hannah."

Albert stood up and walked round the desk as Garner entered the room and said.

"Oh, right. I was wondering why she was not here when I arrived but then I heard what had happened. It's awful."

Garner walked towards Albert's desk and asked.

"Yes, we are looking into what happened to her."

Albert pulled one of the chairs in front of his desk further out and said.

"Please, sit down. I'll help in anyway I can."

He then walked back around his desk and sat down again as Garner took out his notebook and once Albert had sat down again, said.

"I understand Hannah Finley was your secretary."

Albert replied.

"Yes, she's worked for me a few years now. In fact, it must be about ten years."

Garner made some notes and then asked.

"Can you tell me when the last time you saw her was? And where?"

Albert thought for a moment and then replied.

"Sure, it was here yesterday. She was at her desk when I left for the night. I think she mentioned earlier in the day that she was going out with Amy."

He looked at Amy as he said this and as Garner also looked at Amy, she nodded and said.

"That's correct. As I said, we met in Cleethorpes and had a meal together."

Garner added this information to his notebook and then looking back at Albert, said.

"OK, can you confirm where you were yesterday evening?"

Albert replied quickly.

"Yes, I met up with a relative of mine. We had dinner in a restaurant near the library in Cleethorpes and then went for drinks in the pub at the top of Sea View Street."

Garner noted this all down and then asked.

"What time did you leave the area?"

Albert replied.

"Hmmm, not entirely sure but I remember last orders being called and then I walked down the road to get a taxi home. So, I guess it was about eleven."

"OK, can you think of anyone who may want to harm Hannah."

Garner looked at both Albert and Amy as he

spoke, indicating he was asking both of them this question."

Amy replied.

"No, absolutely not. She was liked by everyone as far as I know."

Albert replied.

"The same here. No one comes to mind."

Garner started to get up from his chair and as he did, he asked.

"That's fine then."

Once he was up on his feet and walking towards the door, he turned and said.

"Sorry, should have asked this before. Can you give me the name of the relative you were out with last night?"

Albert replied.

"Sure, it was my cousin Deane Edward's."

# Six

Standing outside Hannah's flat were various officers who were all talking amongst themselves and getting ready to return to their normal police duty's. Inside, there were still some other officers finishing up the search.

Brierton had come out of the bedroom and was looking for the officer who had spoke to her when she arrived earlier. As she looked through the doors along the hallway, she noticed Garner entering the flat through the entrance door. As they saw each other, she said.

"Hello Sir. Any luck at the council offices?"

Garner replied.

"Nothing major, but some useful background stuff about the victim. We can go through it all when we get back to the office. What about here? Found anything?"

Brierton was just about to tell Garner about

the video camera in the bedroom when the officer she was looking for appeared out of a door between herself and Garner. Brierton looked at him and said.

"Ah, there you are. What was it you wanted to speak to me about?"

All three of them moved closer together and the officer held out some evidence bags and said.

"These look like copies of documents from the local council."

Garner took hold of the bags and split them between himself and Brierton. They both looked through them and then Brierton said.

"Odd that someone would have these at home. Especially as they are all invoices and accounting documents. Hannah did not work in the accounts department."

Garner finished looking through the bags he had hold of and said.

"True, let's let everyone finish searching this place and then get everything back to Allan Parsons in the office. He can start processing it all and then we can see where we go from there."

Brierton replied.

"OK, I have one thing to show you in the bedroom before we leave though."

As she spoke, Brierton turned and headed back towards the main bedroom. Garner followed on and once they were both in the bedroom, Brierton led Garner around the bed and to the front of the wardrobe at the end of it. She moved past the door and once she had turned to look at Garner, she pointed to the wardrobe interior. Garner looked inside and then back at Brierton, saying.

"Interesting, what was going on here?"

Brierton replied.

"A video camera and memory cards were found in there. If you stick your head inside, you'll see the mirror is a two-way mirror. It looks like someone, probably Hannah was filming events taking place on the bed."

Garner said.

"OK, where are the memory cards?"

Brierton replied.

"There on their way back to the office with the other items found."

Garner looked at her and with a small amount of cheekiness in his voice said.

"We had better head back then or there'll be no telling what state Parsons will be in."

*****

Just as Garner and Brierton were about to leave the flat another officer came out from inside and called to them.

"Sir, I think you should see this."

Both Garner and Brierton looked back at the officer calling out and waited for them to catch up to where they were standing. The officer carried on speaking once they had arrived beside the two detectives.

"We just found this printed image hidden in a book."

Garner took hold of the image and looked at it and then passed it to Brierton. The picture showed the victim lying naked on her bed with a man lying beside her who was also naked. The picture had the name Albert and a date written on the back of it. As Brierton studied the picture, Garner said.

"I just spoke to him at the council offices. That's Albert Burke, Hannah was his secretary."

Brierton looked at Garner and handed the image back to him. He then passed it back to the other officer.

"Can you get this sent to Allan Parsons at the station. Along with everything else you found."

The officer nodded and turned back towards the flat. As he left Garner and Brierton, Garner called out to him.

"And keep the picture covered. We don't want anyone seeing her like that."

As they walked back to their respective cars, Brierton said.

"One thing that puzzles me about that picture is why would the name of the person with Hannah be written on the back. Surely, she would know who it is."

Garner replied.

"Yeah, I assume the image was taken from video captured using that camera set up found in the wardrobe."

Brierton said.

"I expect so, it looks like the bed in the bedroom with the wardrobe."

Garner said.

"It makes you wonder if there is another person involved with the filming or maybe even a group of people."

Both then walked silently back to their cars and once they had split up, they both made their way back to the station.

# Seven

Parsons was busy at his desk when Brierton walked into the office. She headed straight over to her desk, put her notebook down on it and, after taking he jacket off she sat down and logged onto her computer. As the screen processed her details she looked up at Parsons and said.

"Hiya, how are you doing today?"

Parsons laughed and said.

"I'm fine thanks. What about you? Still a bit hungover?"

Brierton laughed and replied.

"I'm fine, although I think the boss is getting me more black coffee."

Parsons smiled and said.

"I still cannot find out anything about the victim?"

Brierton opened her notebook and looked through it for a moment before saying.

"I suppose it's because she has not had any dealings with us in the past. She has lived and worked in the area for many years but like most people, kept her nose clean."

Parsons said.

"Right, I hear there is a load of stuff coming in from her flat. Any ideas what it is?"

Brierton was typing on her computer now but as she typed she said.

"Yeah, there's loads but I have only seen some paperwork Hannah had at her flat which all seems a bit odd. Hopefully you will be able to make sense of it work out why she had it there. There are also some memory cards that might be linked to some video equipment set up in a wardrobe."

Parsons looked over the office and inquisitively asked.

"Video equipment in a wardrobe. What the?"

Brierton replied.

"Yeah. There was a two-way mirror on the front of the wardrobe that allowed the camera to record her bedtime exploits."

*****

As they both sat talking, both Brierton and Parsons attention was drawn towards the office door as it opened and in walked Garner carrying a cardboard drink carrier in his hand. He rushed into the office and put the carrier down on the first flat surface he came to and reached into his pocket. This was due to his mobile phone ringing within. As he looked at the phone screen he saw it was the stations reception desk calling so he answered the call.

"DCI Garner."

After announcing himself he listened to the caller for a few seconds before saying.

"That's fine, just bring it all up to our office. Allan Parsons is here. He will go through it all and log it into evidence."

After he said this he lowered his mobile and ended the call. He then looked at Parsons and said.

"The stuff from Hannah's flat is here, their

going to bring it up."

Parsons nodded and said.

"OK, I've got things ready here. I'll sort through it and see if there is anything that will help us out.

Garner went and sat down at his own desk now and then realised he had left the drinks sitting on one of the tables near the door so got back up again so he could pass them around. Once again, Garner went to his desk and sat down, saying.

"Right, that's Parsons sorted out for the rest of the day."

He then looked over towards Brierton and said.

"Right, I spoke to Hannah's boss, Albert Burke."

Brierton replied.

"The same Adam Burke in the photo found at her flat."

Garner replied.

"Yes, that's him, although he never

mentioned he was sleeping with Hannah. He did say that he was in the area of the crime scene at the time of the murder. He claims to have been with his cousin. Mind you his cousin is Deane Edward's so we will need to look into his claim further."

Brierton said.

"OK, I'll get hold of everything we have on Burke and Edward's. Is there anyone else we should be looking at?"

*****

Garner spent some time reading through his notes from his visit to the council offices. He wrote down names as he did and then said.

"Yes, Travis Blackburn. He is Hannah's ex husband and apparently it was not a friendly divorce. So, we will need to speak to him at some point. Even if it is just to eliminate him."

Brierton was looking through her own notes now and said.

"I'll add Victor Glenn. With his name being written on that box of memory cards found in the wardrobe. There may be more to his relationship with Hannah other than just at work."

Garner looked over at Brierton and said.

"OK, get all their details and then we will head out and see if we can speak to them."

As they spoke, the door to the office opened and in walked two officers carrying the boxes of items found in Hannah's flat. As they entered, Parsons got up from his desk and walked over to them. He said.

"Can you put them down on this table."

He grabbed the last box sitting on a table against the wall of the office and placed it on the floor underneath the table. Once the table was clear, the officers placed the boxes down and left.

Parsons started to look through the boxes and as he did, said.

"This will take some time to go through but I'll concentrate on the papers found and the video stuff."

Garner replied.

"That sounds good."

He then looked at Brierton and said.

"Do you have those details?"

To which Brierton replied.

"Yes. I have home and work addresses for both and none of them are that far from here."

Garner replied.

"OK, send me the details for Travis Blackburn and I'll go and see him. You visit Victor Glenn and see what he has to say. I would suggest not mentioning the video stuff yet, well, not until Parsons has been through them to see what they contain."

Both Garner and Brierton finished their drinks and then both headed out of the office.

# Eight

Brierton had rung the doorbell of Travis Blackburn's house twice now and was beginning to think there was no one home. But then, she could hear someone opening the door in front of them. As the door opened a slightly bedraggled woman came into view. Holding the door open with one hand and holding a dressing gown closed with the other. Brierton paused for a moment before saying.

"Hello, I'm Detective Sergeant Brierton. I would like to speak to Mr. Travis Blackburn if possible, please."

The woman replied.

"Right, is this about Hannah? We were devastated to hear the news about her."

To which Brierton replied.

"It is. Is Mr. Blackburn here?"

The woman opened the door fully and said.

"Yes, he is, do come in."

Brierton entered the house and once she had passed the woman she closed the door behind them. The woman walked past Brierton and headed into a large living room just off the entrance hall and once in the room she said.

"Please sit down, Travis won't be long. He is just taking a shower. In fact, I should maybe go and get dressed myself."

Once the woman had finished speaking, Brierton said.

"OK, can I get your name please?"

As the woman was leaving the room she looked back and said.

"Not sure why it matters but my name is Bethany Short."

*****

Brierton was left sitting in the living room alone for a few minutes before Travis Blackburn walked into the room. He was closely followed by Bethany who had now got dressed. As they both entered, Brierton stood up and said.

"Hello Mr. Blackburn, my name is Detective Sergeant Brierton."

Blackburn replied as he sat down.

"Hello, I hear this visit is about my ex-wife Hannah. Her friend Amy called earlier and told us the news. It's absolutely dreadful what has happened."

Brierton sat back down and after looking at her notebook, said.

"It is. I'm sorry to have to ask about this but we need to know if you could think of anyone who may have wanted to hurt Hannah?"

Blackburn looked at Brierton and replied.

"Not really. She had gone a bit off the rails since the divorce but what happened to her seems a bit over the top."

Brierton made some notes and then said.

"What do you mean? When you say off the rails."

Blackburn thought for a moment and then said.

"Well, she took the divorce very badly."

Bethany laughed and chipped in at this point by saying, sharply.

"Not sure why she took it so badly when it was her who wanted the divorce."

Blackburn looked momentarily at Bethany and then looked back towards Brierton said.

"True, but it was because she found out we had been sleeping together."

# Nine

Victor Glenn was sitting at his desk when Garner knocked on the office door and pushed it open. As he walked into the office Victor stopped what he was doing and looked up towards the door. As Garner came into view, Victor said.

"Hello. Can I help you?"

Garner walked across the office floor and as he arrived at the desk where Victor was sitting, took out his leather warrant card holder and opened it. He held the card holder out in front of himself so Victor could see it and said.

"Hello, I'm DCI Garner. Sorry to just walk in but there was no one at the desk outside."

Victor studied the identification card and said.

"No problem, Alison is probably away doing something. How can I help you?"

Garner put his identification card back in his pocket and said.

"I am here to talk to you about Hannah Finley. You may not be aware but we found her this morning near the promenade in Cleethorpes. She has been killed."

Victor took on a stunned look and said nothing in reply to what he had been told. Garner noticed Victor seemed to be looking past him and back towards the office door. So, Garner turned and as he did, he became aware there was a woman standing near the open door. She had heard what had been said and looked shocked as she said.

"Are you talking about Hannah who worked here?"

Garner could see the woman was a bit unsteady on her feet and looked around the office for a chair. He spotted one near the desk so grabbed it and carried it over to where she was standing. Placing the chair to her side Garner said.

"Here, sit down."

As the woman sat down, Victor said.

"This is Alison, my secretary. She was a

friend as well as a colleague of Hannah's."

Garner looked back towards Victor as Alison sat down and nodded. Then, looking back at Alison, he said.

"How's that?"

Alison looked at Garner and replied.

"Fine thanks. Just a bit of a shock. I'll take a moment and then get back to my desk."

Garner moved his attention back towards Victor and said.

"I understand you have been seeing Alison outside of the office. Can you tell me how long you had been seeing her?"

Victor said.

"Oh right. Not sure where you got that from but it's not really what it looks like. We had been out together on a couple of occasions but more as friends really. She had been having problems with her ex-husband and just wanted a distraction from time to time."

Garner had now taken his notebook out of another pocket and was making some notes when Victor said.

"Alison, if you are feeling OK, could you go back to your desk and close the door please."

Garner waited and watched as Alison got up from the chair and left the office. Once she had done as asked and closed the door, Garner picked up the chair Alison had been sitting on and carried it back to the desk where Victor was sitting. Garner lowered the chair back to the ground and once he had adjusted its angle at the desk, sat down on it in anticipation of what he was about to be told. Once Garner had settled, Victor said.

"Look, I'm horrified to hear what has happened to Hannah, but I would hate for what was going on between us to be misunderstood or taken for something it was not."

Garner looked at his notebook and held his pen towards it and paused. The movement had the desired affect on Victor who carried on speaking.

"The truth is Hannah had invited me out a few months ago. I knew she had been through a nasty divorce because she made no secret about it around the office. We went out for a meal and ended up back at my place. Once thing led to another and she stayed over. We did the same thing a couple more times but that's all."

Victor paused as Garner made some notes and then continued.

"So, there's nothing more to it. It was just two people meeting up from time to time for some fun."

Once Victor had finished speaking and Garner had finished making some notes, Garner said.

"OK, that's fine. A couple of last things I need to ask."

Victor replied.

"Sure, ask away."

Garner flicked back through his notebook to see what time Amy had last seen Hannah and then asked.

"Can you tell me where you were last night at about eight o'clock?"

Victor replied quickly.

"That's an easy one, although maybe a bit embarrassing considering what I just told you. I was at home with my wife. She works away a lot but is home at the moment."

Garner updated his notebook and then asked.

"OK, I will need to speak to her to confirm that, have you got her contact details, please?"

Victor took a piece of paper from his desk an wrote down his wife's contact details. As he passed the paper to Garner, Garner said.

"Last thing I need to ask is, can you think of anyone who may want to harm Hannah?"

Victor just shook his head it this question.

Garner answered this by saying.

"OK, that's all for now. If I need to speak to you again I will let you know."

He then got up out of his chair and made his way towards the office door, which he opened and left the office through.

*****

As Garner left Victor Glenn's office he entered the area outside where Alison was now sitting behind her desk. As he walked past her she said.

"It's terrible what has happened to Hannah. She was a lovely person who had a bright future ahead of her now she had got away from her cheating husband. Still, I doubt he will be losing much sleep now he gets to keep his money."

Garner stopped in his tracks as Alison spoke and moved to the front of her desk and said.

"What do you mean?"

Alison replied.

"I have known Hannah for a long time and before she got married to Travis, she told me he had insisted on her signing a prenup."

Garner took this in and then said.

"I see. Do you know any of the details of the prenup."

Alison said.

"Not really, I maybe should not have said

anything at all. But, she did say she was due a large payout if he committed adultery."

He then turned away from Alison's desk and headed out of the office and back to the station.

# Ten

The builder's yard where Deane Edward's ran his business from was almost deserted when Brierton arrived. She pulled into a small parking area just inside the main gate which was wide open and parked her car next to a marked police car that had arrived shortly before she had. The officers in the marked car had been called to the yard in support of her visit.

Once she got out of her car she started to look around. She quickly spotted a portable cabin office with a sign stating it was the reception and offices area, so she walked across the parking area towards the cabin. As she approached the cabin, a door at one end of it opened and a familiar face appeared.

It was Freddy Woods, the chap she had met when she visited the council offices with Garner earlier in the day. He spotted her walking towards the door so stopped and waited for her to get to him before saying.

"Hello again. Can I help you?"

Brierton stopped walking once she was standing next to him and replied.

"Maybe. I need to speak to Mr. Edward's. Is he here?"

Freddy grabbed hold of the door and pulled it fully open again and said.

"Yeah, he's inside. Go on in."

*****

Brierton walked past him and through the door. She soon arrived at what appeared to be an open-plan type of office area. There did not appear to be any separate offices inside the cabin and as she walked in, she saw Deane Edward's sitting at a desk in the corner of the room. He looked up as he heard Brierton enter and said.

"Hello. Can I help you?"

As soon as he finished speaking, he realised he recognised Brierton and spoke again sharply.

"Hang on. I know you, don't I? You're the police."

Brierton said.

"That's right. I'm Detective Sergeant Brierton. I would like to speak to you about Hannah Finley."

Edward's stood up and walked around the desk. He stood right in front of Brierton in what seemed to be an attempt to intimidate her and said.

"Right, yes, Hannah. Lovely girl. I heard what happened to her, but I don't see why you need to speak to me. I was one of the few people that knew her but hadn't slept with her."

Brierton was a bit shocked by what he said. Not so much the aggressive nature of him because he was known to the police as a thug, they would love to put in prison but had never managed to get enough evidence to do it. So, she just replied.

"OK, I'll make a note of that. What I want to know is if you can tell me about your whereabouts on the evening she was killed?"

Edward's thought for a moment and said.

"Easy, I was in Cleethorpes with my cousin

Albert. We had a meal and then went for a couple of drinks at the top of Sea View Street. I then drove home."

Brierton said.

"Can you confirm what time you were at the pub?"

Edward's thought for a moment and then spoke with some arrogance in his voice.

"Yeah, I think it was around nine o'clock. Cannot be sure though, I was a bit pissed to be honest."

He laughed as he carried on speaking.

"I suppose it was lucky for me you lot are not very good in the evenings or I might have been nicked."

Brierton just smiled at his comments. He was known for his attitude towards the police but Brierton had dealt with much worse over the years so just took it in her stride. She had now taken her notebook out and was writing down everything he said and once she had done so, she said.

"Right, OK. How well did you know Hannah Finley then? I guess not very well if you had not managed to charm her into bed with you."

Edward's was not happy with this slight. Which is exactly why Brierton had said it. She new how to push the buttons of people like Edward's and the effect it would have on him. She was right, he took on a more aggressive pose and said, angrily.

"I really didn't know her at all and wouldn't have touched it if she turned up in front of me naked."

He then retreated back around his desk and sat back down again. He looked at Brierton and said.

"If that's all. Unlike you, I have work to get on with."

Brierton decided to ask a couple of more questions because she could see she had rattled him. She said.

"So, I guess you won't know of anyone who may want to hurt Hannah?"

He just looked sternly at her and replied.

"No. Is that it now?"

Brierton smiled back at him and said.

"No, I think that is it for now. Although, I'm sure I will be speaking to you again at some point in the future."

Edward's responded to this by just saying nothing and lowering his head down towards his desk. He picked up some paperwork and started to read it. He muttered.

"You see yourself out."

# Eleven

Once inside the Glenn's house, Garner and Brierton were led into a large kitchen to the rear of the house by Jenna. Both Garner and Brierton had identified themselves and Jenna had obviously been tipped off they were going to be visiting so they had not been kept hanging around on the doorstep for long.

Once they all came to a standstill in the kitchen, Jenna asked.

"So, how can I help you?"

Garner took out his notebook and flicked back through a couple of pages and then said.

"We spoke to your husband earlier and he said he was here with you yesterday evening and night. We just need to be able to confirm the details he gave us. Can you confirm that you were together?"

Jenna responded very quickly.

"Yes, we were here all evening and went to bed at about ten. Why do you need to know that?"

Brierton replied.

"We are investigating the unexplained death of Hannah Finley. We are speaking to everyone who knew her, either on a personal basis or through her work at the council."

Jenna thought for a moment before responding.

"So, are you saying you think my husband had something to do with her death?"

Garner made some notes as Jenna spoke and replied to her question.

"No, just asking the same questions to everyone involved in Hannah's work and private lives. In as much to eliminate them as much as anything else. We'll be on our way now. Thanks for your time."

Jenna started to make her way back to the front of the house and as the three of them made their way through the house and along the hallway, Brierton noticed some photographs on the wall of the hallway. She said.

"Are these photos of you and your husband?"

Jenna stopped and joining Brierton in looking at the photos said.

"Yes, we met while both serving in the Army."

Garner joined the others and while looking at the pictures said.

"Who's this in this photo?"

Garner was pointing to a photograph which had three people in. He was just looking for confirmation really as he recognised the third person in the photo with the Glenns. Sure enough, Jenna confirmed who the other person was.

"That's Dean Edwards. He served in the same unit as us and lives around here."

Garner replied.

"Yes, I thought that's who it was. We've met a few times."

Jenna laughed a bit and said.

"Doesn't surprise me. He has always been getting into trouble one way or another. Him and Victor are as thick as thieves."

Jenna paused and then said.

"Oops, I should probably not say that to you."

Brierton and Garner both looked at Jenna while Brierton said.

"Probably not."

Garner turned back towards the front door and pushing down the door handle, pulled the door towards him so they could leave. As Brierton followed Garner out of the door she said.

"We will get in touch if we need to speak to you further."

Jenna watched them walk down the garden path before closing the door behind them. She then went back into the kitchen and picked up her mobile phone. After tapping on the screen of the smart phone she put it too her ear and once the call was connected she said.

"That's the police been and gone. I told

them you were here all night but they never asked who else was here so I never said anything."

She paused while the other person spoke and then she ended the call by saying.

"OK, we will need to have a chat about your shenanigans as I'm getting fed up with covering for you."

She then ended the call and put her phone back down on the kitchen counter.

# Twelve

"Sorry to keep you waiting."

Both Garner and Brierton turned towards an opening door as they heard these words being called out. Rachel Howton appeared through the door and walked towards them. As she did, Garner and Brierton stood up and waited for Howton to join them. Howton had carried out the post-mortem on Hannah and had the results in the folder she was carrying. As she joined the two waiting for her she said.

"Right, come through here and I'll explain what I've found."

She walked straight past Garner and Brierton and headed towards another door at the side of the waiting area of the mortuary. This door led to a small office that had some chairs and a table set within. The room was usually used as a private area for relatives to wait when a loved one had passed away and they needed to complete some paperwork. Once they were all inside the room, Howton closed the door and said.

"Come on then, site down."

Obeying this order, both Garner and Brierton pulled chairs out from under the table and quickly sat down. Howton sat down on another chair and placed her folder on the table in front of her. As she opened the folder she said.

"I have sent a copy of these results through the mail system but I wanted to talk to you about them as well."

Garner replied.

"OK, what did you find?"

Howton started to read through the notes in the folder and as she did, she started to speak.

"Most of the results confirm that she had eaten a curry shortly before dying. Her stomach contents proved that and the fact she had not fully digested it."

She paused as she read some more and then continued.

"There were also some traces of alcohol in her blood. But, not enough to suggest she was drunk and may have simply fallen over the small fence at the top of the waterfall."

Garner interrupted Howton at this point and said.

"So, cause of death?"

Howton looked at him and then towards Brierton and said.

"Always in a hurry isn't he."

Brierton just smiled at this. She didn't bother answering as she knew this was a rhetorical question.

Howton carried on.

"It looks like her neck was broken which I think was the cause of death but, other bruises give us an insight to what happened."

Howton paused once more and pulled a piece of paper out of the folder. She then started to read from it.

"The bruises I found on the victim's upper body suggest that she was grabbed from behind. There is not extensive bruising around her neck which suggests the action of killing her was done in a sharp movement. You know, like military people do to kill someone quickly and quietly. Bruises found on other parts of her body look like she was then lifted and thrown over the railing at the top of the waterfall. Other cuts on her head and body were caused by the fall into the pool."

Brierton said.

"So, she was definitely dead before falling into the water?"

Howton looked at Brierton and said.

"Yes, no indication of being alive as she entered the water so she was dead before going down the waterfall."

Garner and Brierton stared at each other as they had both realised almost everyone they had spoken to up till now regarding Hannah's death, had a military background.

# Thirteen

Having made their way back to the office, Garner and Brierton were now waiting for an update from Parsons about the items found in Hannah's flat by the search team. Once they had all settled in their seats around a table in the office, Parson's started to talk.

"Right, I have been through all the paperwork found at Hannah Finley's flat and from what I can see, there has been a bit of a scam working within the building works department."

As he spoke, he passed a copy of the folder he was reading from, to Garner who opened it, so both himself and Brierton could read the contents. Parsons then carried on.

"If you look at the first couple of pages, you can see a list of invoices between the council and Deane Edwards building company. Now, you will see that a lot of the invoices on those pages refer to the same properties. The thing is. Some of the invoices seem to be for the same work carried out multiple times."

While Brierton carried on reading, she asked.

"So, does it look like the work is invoiced at reasonable rates, but multiple times for the same work."

Parsons replied.

"Yes. I have not checked yet but I am guessing that invoices for much higher amounts would trigger checks to be carried out by the council accounts department, whereas multiple invoices for duplicate work would not be picked up."

Garner replied.

"Would it help if the person in charge of the accounts department within the council was involved?"

Parsons thought for a moment and looking at Garner, said.

"I would guess so, they could probably block further checks being made into what may be going on."

Garner said.

"Right, once we are finished here, pass everything we have on this to the fraud guys. They may be able to use it for further investigations into what may be going on."

*****

Parsons moved all the paperwork to one side and then slid Hannah Finley's phone and the box of memory cards in front of himself. He placed his hand on the top of the box and said.

"Now, the cards in here have all been uploaded to the system and I have watched all of them. The label on the box suggests the footage contained images of both the Glenn's, but in fact, they only show Victor Glenn with Hannah. The videos leave nothing to the imagination but do not appear to show any form of crime taking place."

Brierton said.

"OK, what about the phone?"

Parsons replied.

"That's a different kettle of fish altogether.

There are more intimate images on it that show Hannah was involved in sexual relationships with both Victor Glenn and Albert Burke. But like the videos, everything seems to be consensual."

Brierton said.

"So, they give us nothing we weren't already aware of then?"

Parsons pushed a piece of paper towards Brierton and said.

"Not really, apart from this."

Brierton picked up the piece of paper and started to read it.

Garner said.

"What is it?"

While Brierton was reading, Parsons said.

"It's a printout of a text message that was on the phone. It says, if Hannah opens her mouth about things, she will regret it."

Brierton finished reading the message and passed it over to Garner who started to read it. As he did, he said.

"Well. I guess we need to speak to Edward's again. About this and the discrepancy with the time he and Albert Burke claimed they left the pub."

# Fourteen

It had not taken long for Garner and Brierton to arrive at the builders yard of Deane Edwards. So, they parked up in the area outside the office cabin and got out of the car. They both looked around the yard and could not help but notice there was no one about. So, they headed for the office cabin and entered through the door which was already open. As they entered and walked along the corridor to the office area Garner called out.

"Hello, it's the Police."

No answer was heard and as they entered the office, what sounded like someone running around the outside of the cabin could be heard. A pair of large glass doors opposite the entrance to the office where Garner and Brierton were entering through were open. It was this that allowed the sound of someone running could be heard and as they looked towards the desk that Edward's had been sitting behind when Brierton last visited him, they both saw there was a body slumped over the desk.

Garner said.

"Check him out."

As he spoke, he quickly left the office through the glass doors to see if he could see who had gone out of them and run away. Unfortunately, because whoever had left the office had gotten a few seconds of a head start on him, Garner could see no one outside the office. So, he returned inside and walked across to where Brierton was looking for any signs of life as she looked up at him and shook her head.

Garner said.

"Is it Edward's?"

Brierton looked at him and just nodded. Garner replied to this.

"Right, we had better call it in and get the area sealed off."

Brierton looked at Garner and nodded. So, Garner took out his mobile phone and called back to the station's control room to get more units and a crime scene team down as soon as possible.

*****

Garner and Brierton had waited while other officers had setup a cordon around the cabin, where the office containing Edward's body was found. Once they thought the crime scene team had had enough time to make their initial examination, they both approached the entrance door again. The door was now being guarded by a uniformed officer who turned towards them as they approached and said.

"If you want to enter, you'll need to suit up first as their still processing the scene."

Both took a few minutes to get into the suits they had been given, and once ready they entered the cabin through the entrance door. Brierton led the way, as she had been here before and knew to go straight along the short corridor then into the main office area. Once there, Howton could be seen examining a body sitting in the chair and slumped over the desk where Brierton had spoken to him earlier. As they both advanced towards the desk, Howton looked up and said.

"Hello, we meet again."

Garner walked a little way around the desk

and said.

"Hi, I wish we could stop meeting like this."

Howton laughed and said.

"Then we would both be out of work, wouldn't we."

While Garner and Howton were talking, Brierton started looking around the office. She said.

"Is there any reason to hold off searching here?"

Howton replied to Brierton.

"No, it looks like he was strangled from behind while sitting at his desk. There are no signs of a fight or much resistance really so I am working on the theory that he knew his attacker and they knew exactly what they were doing."

Garner replied.

"So, some sort of professional killing?"

Howton looked at Garner and said.

"Yes. Although strangulation is not the most

common method used by professional killers."

Garner said.

"Well, with the sort of people he was involved with, we will probably have a couple of volumes of possible killers."

Howton carried on examining the body as Garner said this and Brierton started to look through the various filing cabinets lining one of the office walls. As she opened a drawer and looked inside she said.

"I think we will need to get some more hands in here. It will take ages to look through all this stuff."

Garner walked back around the desk and started looking in drawers as well. He said.

"I'll go and get some of the guys outside to come in and help."

He then left the office and Howton said.

"Is this chap part of another investigation?"

Brierton turned and said.

"Yeah, a few to be honest. But presently the

Hannah Finley murder case."

As they spoke, Garner walked back into the office followed by five uniformed officers and once they were all in the room he stopped and said.

"Right, I want you to go through everything in here and everything that looks like it is linked to council work, get it sent to Allan Parsons at the station."

Once he had given these instructions, all the officers spread out throughout the office and started to search through everything.

# Fifteen

After a short time, the front door opened and Victor Glenn appeared in the doorway. Brierton looked at him and said.

"Hi, can I come in and have a quick chat, please?"

Victor opened the door fully and using his arm, beckoned her inside and closed the door behind her. As soon as they were both stood in the hallway of the house Brierton asked.

"Is your wife here?"

Victor looked along the hallway and said.

"Yes, she's in the living room. Do you want to speak to her as well?"

Brierton replied.

"No, I need to talk to you alone first."

Victor said.

"OK, this is all intriguing. Lets got through to the kitchen."

As they both walked through the house, Brierton took out her notebook in preparation for their chat. Once they were in the kitchen she closed the door and started to speak.

"We carried out a search of Hannah's flat and retrieved several images and videos. Some of them were of an intimate nature and showed yourself being intimate with her. Now, we also found details of what looked like a plan to blackmail you regarding these images. Can you tell me if you ever received any threats regarding these images?"

Victor answered her question instantly.

"I think I should call Jenna through at this point as she was fully aware of my relationship with Hannah."

Brierton nodded and waited while Victor opened the kitchen door and called out.

"Jen, can you come through please?"

*****

Once Jenna had joined them in the kitchen, Victor said.

"Sorry about this, but DS Brierton here has something I think is best discussed with both of us."

He looked at Brierton and said.

"Please carry on Detective Sergeant."

Brierton looked at Jenna and repeated what she had said to her husband.

"As I told your husband, we found some videos and images while looking through Hannah's flat that show her and himself in some very intimate situations. We also found evidence that she was going to or already was blackmailing him regarding these images and videos."

Jenna stopped Brierton carrying on speaking by saying.

"Ah, right. She was obviously not aware of our personal arrangements. As you know we met while serving in the Army and have been together as a couple since then. The thing is that because we were not married until we left the armed forces we were often posted long distances apart. Now, because we both have, lets just say, needs, we agreed that other sexual partners are allowable. Since we left the Army and got married, this agreement has stayed in place due to my work, that carries on taking me away for long periods of time."

Brierton said.

"So, are you saying that you knew about your husbands relationship with Hannah?"

Jenna looked at her husband and then back towards Brierton and said.

"Totally, so there would be no point in trying to blackmail Victor as I already knew about them sleeping together."

Brierton wrote all this down in her notebook and then asked.

"Would there be any repercussions for you both if she had released the details of the relationship into the public domain. Would that cause you any problems on the personal front or even from a business point of view?"

The Glenn's looked at each other and seemed to think for a bit. They then both looked at Brierton before Victor spoke.

"Not really, these sorts of things stir up some news space for a bit but I am not really that well known so I wouldn't see it playing out in the press for very long."

Once he had finished speaking, Brierton turned and looked at Jenna and waited to see if she had anything to add. All Jenna said was.

"Same here, not sure it would even make the news locally really."

# Sixteen

The stations reception had called Garner to tell him he had a visitor, so he returned to the station, leaving Brierton to finish looking through Edward's office with the other officers. Once he got back to the station, he headed for one of the interview rooms where Travis Blackburn and his solicitor had been sitting for a while, waiting. Garner joined them in the room and sat down opposite them and said.

"Right, how can I help you."

Travis's solicitor started to speak while passing a piece of paper forward across the table towards Garner.

"My client contacted me as he was concerned that he is being considered as a suspect in his ex-wife's murder because there was a prenup signed before their marriage. We wanted to pop in and disclose a clause in the prenup that hopefully will help you see he should not be a suspect."

Garner took the paper and spun it around so he could read it and as he did, he said.

"OK, that makes sense."

The piece of paper Garner was reading was a statement from the solicitors regarding a clause that said. If Hannah died between them splitting up and the agreed amount being paid to her, then the same amount would be split between two local charities.

As Garner read, Travis said.

"So, to be fair, the people running these charities are more likely to be involved in her death than me. I have nothing to gain."

Garner looked at Travis and nodded and the solicitor sitting beside Travis said.

"To be fair, you should have known this clause existed if you had read the copy of the prenup that Hannah should have had in her possession."

Garner looked at the solicitor and replied.

"We have never seen it."

Garner shifted his attention to Travis and carried on.

"Where do you think her copy would be? We have been through her flat and I don't recall it being mentioned."

Travis replied.

"I'm sure it should have been there. Although we were getting divorced, we were still talking and we looked through it only a couple of weeks ago to ensure I was going along with the terms."

Garner placed the piece of paper he had been given into the folder he had with him and started to stand up. He said.

"Thanks for this, I appreciate you popping in and drawing our attention to it. I'll look into why it was not at the flat."

Garner picked up his folder and headed out of the interview room.

# Seventeen

Brierton watched the CCTV footage Parsons had sent on to her covering the period Albert admitted he had left the pub. She watched as he came out of the pub and walked through the Armed forces memorial gate and down to the promenade. He could then be seen walking along the promenade towards the Pier. Once she finished watching him leave the promenade by walking up from the Pier and into the market area, she looked up and said.

"Well, that's Albert Burke accounted for. The CCTV shows him leaving the pub as stated and making his way to the market area from the promenade. At no point does he enter the gardens."

Garner was now back in the office and passing the details of the prenup to Parsons to record. As Brierton spoke he looked over towards her and asked.

"What about the time? Edward's claimed it was earlier than Burke had claimed."

Brierton looked once more at her screen and replied.

"No, Burke was telling the truth about the time. I imagine, Edward's was just trying to be a jerk towards us as usual."

Garner said.

"OK, so that kind of clears him really."

Brierton replied.

"I'm afraid it does. Although to me, he had a strong motive for wanting her dead."

Garner said.

"I am not going to cross him off the list of people involved though. There is still the business of the works scam that still appears to be behind all of this."

After speaking, both Garner and Brierton returned to looking through their notes.

*****

The team were all feeling a bit deflated now. This was because everyone who had a motive for Hannah's death was able to account for their whereabouts at the time of the killing. Garner and Brierton were sitting at their desks reading through their notes while Parsons was sitting at his desk looking through all the CCTV he had now been sent. Once he had done so he said.

"I have got the CCTV footage from inside the restaurant and the cameras outside along the street."

He then got up from his desk and moved a larger screen that was sitting in the corner of the room and positioned it so they could all watch it.

Garner and Brierton both moved across the office and grabbed chairs in front of the screen in preparation to watch the footage again. Parsons clicked his mouse and the videos started to play. As they watched they saw the same people coming and going from the restaurant but a new thing caught Brierton's eye. She quickly spoke up.

"Hang on, can you go back a bit."

Parsons stopped the video and started to slowly rewind it in a way that they could watch it but in reverse. Brierton got up from her seat and stood much closer to the screen and watched intently. When the video got to the point that she thought she saw something she said.

"Hold it there."

Parsons stopped the video. Garner and Parsons waited while Brierton studied it closely. After a short while, she pointed to the screen and said.

"Look, there's someone outside the window looking in."

Garner got up from his seat and moved alongside Brierton so he could look closer at the screen. He turned back towards Parsons and said.

"Can you zoom in on the area of the window?"

Parsons turned his attention to his computer screen and started to click his mouse. He looked up and said.

"How's that?"

Both Garner and Brierton looked closer at the screen and what seemed to be within a millisecond Brierton said.

"I cannot be sure because I can't make out

the face. But the build, coat and hat remind me of Amy Strong's boyfriend. Do you remember? The guy who was in her office the first time we went there. I think his name was Freddy."

Garner took a closer look at the screen and said.

"You might just be right."

He looked at Parsons and said.

"Can you get all the footage from the cameras in the area and see if you can trace the movements of that person."

Parsons nodded and started clicking away with his mouse while studying his screen.

*****

After a while, Parsons looked up from his screen and said.

"Right, I've got all the footage showing the movements of the person in the window. None of it shows the persons face but it is obvious it's the same person."

Brierton got up from her desk and made her way back to Parsons desk where she sat down beside him. Garner moved back to the large screen so he could watch. Once they were all settled, Parsons had compiled the footage into one long video so viewing it would be easier and had positioned the start at the point the person had been seen outside the restaurant. He started the video and made it rewind at triple speed to the beginning when the person was first picked up on CCTV walking down Bentley Street towards the shops. The three of them watched as the person of interest appeared out of Bentley Street and crossed over St Peters Avenue, before disappearing into the market area. For some reason, there was no coverage in the market area. As they continued to watch, Parsons remarked.

"I have requested details as to why there is no footage in the market area and if there are any known private cameras there that could help us out."

Garner nodded at Parsons as he continued watching.

The next time the person was seen on screen was via footage from the library cameras. The video showed the person arriving at the restaurant on the corner of Albert Road. They stood near one of the windows that enabled them to look into the restaurant but because it was darker outside than within, they could not be seen very well from inside. This was the point in the footage that Brierton had spotted the outline of the person waiting outside.

Parsons paused the video and said.

"Along with the request for footage from the market area, I have also asked for a team of officers to pop along the other end of Bentley Street and ask residents for any doorbell footage that may indicate where the person came from before we first saw them.

Garner looked at Parsons and replied.

"Good idea, well done."

Parsons then restarted the video and they all watched intently because they all hoped that the video would now help them see if this person was someone they should be looking at closely as a possible suspect for Hannah's murder. Parsons stuck with the footage from the library at this point because Hannah and Amy could be seen leaving through the window but it also showed the person outside moving away from the window and into a shadowed area to the side of the building. As Hannah and

Amy split up and headed towards their respective cars, the person watching them crossed the road as well and followed Hannah into the Pier Gardens.

Parsons once again had to say.

"There are no working cameras within the garden area so we don't have anything showing the actual attack. But we are certain the attack took place within the gardens because we have no sign of Hannah leaving the area but if you watch the next bit, we can see someone dressed the same as the person who followed Hannah into the gardens walking down Sea View Street about ten minutes later."

Garner replied.

"Right, OK. I'm guessing there will be some footage from down there as I know there is at least one taxi company and various bars. Are there officers down there looking?"

Parsons said.

"Yes, I'm waiting for them to get back to me."

Garner looked over to Brierton and said.

"Right, I think we should bring this Freddy guy in for a chat."

Brierton nodded in agreement with what Garner had said and then added.

"What about Amy? If he knew where they were going to be, then maybe she is more involved than we realised."

Garner looked at Brierton and replied.

"I think you may be right. Let's bring them both in."

# Eighteen

Because Amy had called into work in the morning and told them she was taking a couple of days off, the task of finding her so she could be brought into the station looked like it was going to be hard. Police officers had called at her house but there was no sign of her there. Her neighbours said they had seen her in the morning getting into her car having placed a suitcase in the boot.

The officers who went to her address called back to the station to pass this information onto Garner and his team. This led to a 'be on the lookout' order being issued for Amy and her vehicle. The team hoped it would not be too long until she was located and arrested.

*****

Freddy on the other hand was located much quicker. His car had been spotted in a car park behind the market in Freeman Street, so the area was being searched by a large group of officers and all CCTV operators were assisting with the search.

It was not long before he was spotted walking back towards his car and challenged by officers. He tried to make a break for it by jumping up on a wall that led to the back of one of the shops but was grabbed by an officer. Another officer quickly joined in to assist with the arrest and said.

"Crikey, that was close."

The second officer replied.

"It was. If he had of got up there, we would have spent the next two days trying to get him down and probably dodging roof tiles."

Both officers laughed as they got up and pulled Freddy up to his feet.

*****

A couple of hours later, Amy was being led into the police custody area in the station. She had tried to get out of the area but her car was spotted by the automated number plate recognition system. Traffic police were alerted to her location and she was arrested.

*****

Although Garner didn't know it yet, the case was just about to be blown wide open. Amy had been brought into the station and was sitting in an interview room with her legal adviser, waiting for Garner to join them. He eventually walked in and sat down opposite them both and placed his case folder on the table in front of himself. As he settled, he opened the folder and took a photograph out. It was the image of who he believed to be Freddy Wood standing outside the window of the restaurant.

He pushed the picture forwards across the table and spun it round once it was in front of Amy. He asked.

"Do you know who this is?"

As he asked he watched the colour drain from Amy's face as she looked at the picture. She looked up at her adviser and then at Garner. She pushed the picture back towards Garner and said.

"I'm in a lot of trouble, aren't I?"

Garner put the picture back in his folder and said.

"Well, we think the person in the picture is your boyfriend, Freddy Wood. Now the question is, how did he know where you and Hannah would be at that precise time? Can you shed some light on that?"

Amy was now as pale as could be and once again looked at her adviser and then said.

"It is Freddy. It's not so much that I told him where we would be, but Deane Edwards told me where to take Hannah. He said he was arranging for her to be scared off from going public about the stuff at work."

Amy's adviser said.

"Right stop right there. I think I should speak to my client before this interview goes any further."

Garner replied.

"OK, that's probably a good idea because she is looking at a conspiracy to murder charge alongside Freddy."

*****

Freddy was sitting in an interview room with Brierton and another officer. Garner joined them and sat down opposite Freddy. He looked at Brierton and said.

"Amy is in another room and has confirmed the person in the CCTV image is Freddy so I think we can just get him charged for Hannah's murder as well."

Freddy said.

"What? You cannot blame Amy for what happened."

Brierton replied to this.

"Well. Tell us everything and if what you say is true, she will get a lesser charge."

Freddy looked at his adviser and said.

"I'm just going to tell them what happened because it's not fair that Amy gets any of the blame."

He then looked back at Garner and Brierton and started to talk.

"Amy was told by Deane Edwards to take Hannah out for a meal. He told her when and where to take her. He told me to wait outside and when Hannah left Amy, I was to kill her."

Brierton said.

"Just like that. Are you really that cold and callous?"

Freddy replied.

"No, of course not but Deane told me we could all end up in prison if she talked about the building works deal between himself, Burke and the Glenn's."

With Freddy confessing to the killing of Hannah and then going onto admit it was him that had also killed Edward's. It pretty much meant the case would soon be closed but Garner had one last thing to ask.

"Can you tell us why you killed Edward's?"

Freddy looked back at Garner and said.

"Well, I guess it doesn't really matter why now. He wanted me to kill Amy as well so we could all get a bigger cut of the money. But I figured out the others involved in the scam wanted more for themselves. So, it would not be long before I was in the way as well."

Garner wanted to clear up a couple of loose ends before ending the interview. He looked through his notebook and asked.

"While looking through Hannah's flat we found various documents. It has come to our attention that a copy of her prenup should have been there but was not. Can you shed any light on this matter?"

Freddy replied.

"That's easy. Amy removed it to make you look at her ex-husband as a possible suspect."

Garner noted this down and then asked.

"And finally, you have no military background but killed both Hannah and Edward's using military killing techniques. Can you explain how you knew these techniques?"

Freddy responded.

"You should look into some of the training Jenna Glenn provides."

# Nineteen

Once Amy and Freddy had been charged. Garner had told Brierton and Parsons to head home for some rest. He told them they could finish all the tidying up of the case the next day. Parsons headed straight out of the office and shortly after, Garner and Brierton left the building. As they walked across the car park towards their cars, Garner and Brierton talked about the future and where they saw themselves going. Brierton now had all the qualifications required to move up to Inspector, either as a detective or into a uniformed position. As they walked, Garner said.

"Have you had any initial thoughts about what you may do next?"

Brierton thought briefly and said.

"Not really but, I feel I want to take on more of my own cases. The problem is that there are no positions here for me to move into."

Garner laughed and replied.

"True, us old git's never seem to move on or retire do we."

Once they had both stopped laughing at this statement, Garner continued with.

"To be fair. I am getting tired of all of this. We seem to be getting more and more cases but working with less and less support."

Brierton nodded in agreement at this and responded by saying.

"What about yourself? Will you carry on or can I have your job?"

Garner laughed again and said.

"You never know. I think my daughter is coming home soon, she has been working with animals overseas for the last few years. I am hoping to persuade her to stay here and open a wildlife sanctuary in Grimsby."

Brierton looked at Garner and said.

"Do you think that is a possibility? I know she has been away for years. You must miss her a lot."

"We do, so, I'm hoping she will stick around for a while. So, you never know, you may get my job and Grimsby will get its long-needed Giraffe Rescue centre."

As he finished speaking, both started to laugh more and made their way to their respective cars to head home.

# About the Author

John Messingham was born in Hampton, Middlesex, England. After finishing school, he joined the British Army and served as an Infantryman and later trained as a radio operator within the battalion mortar platoon. After his time in the army, he trained as a computer programmer and started a long career in IT. The fiction he writes sometimes draws on both his military and IT backgrounds.

For more information about John and his writing, please visit:
https://johnmessingham.co.uk

**DCI Garner and DS Brierton
Murder Mysteries**

**Series One**
The Pier
The Body in the Van
Murder in the Park

**Series Two**
Murder in the Mill
Woodland Murder
Death in the Gardens

**Short Stories**
Murder on the Mince Pie Special

Printed in Great Britain
by Amazon